W9-DDO-142

Dear Parents:

Congratulations! Your child is taking the first steps on an exciting journey. The destination? Independent reading!

STEP INTO READING® will help your child get there. The program offers five steps to reading success. Each step includes fun stories and colorful art or photographs. In addition to original fiction and books with favorite characters, there are Step into Reading Non-Fiction Readers, Phonics Readers and Boxed Sets, Sticker Readers, and Comic Readers—a complete literacy program with something to interest every child.

Learning to Read, Step by Step!

Ready to Read   Preschool–Kindergarten
• big type and easy words • rhyme and rhythm • picture clues
For children who know the alphabet and are eager to begin reading.

Reading with Help   Preschool–Grade 1
• basic vocabulary • short sentences • simple stories
For children who recognize familiar words and sound out new words with help.

Reading on Your Own   Grades 1–3
• engaging characters • easy-to-follow plots • popular topics
For children who are ready to read on their own.

Reading Paragraphs   Grades 2–3
• challenging vocabulary • short paragraphs • exciting stories
For newly independent readers who read simple sentences with confidence.

Ready for Chapters   Grades 2–4
• chapters • longer paragraphs • full-color art
For children who want to take the plunge into chapter books but still like colorful pictures.

STEP INTO READING® is designed to give every child a successful reading experience. The grade levels are only guides; children will progress through the steps at their own speed, developing confidence in their reading. The F&P Text Level on the back cover serves as another tool to help you choose the right book for your child.

Remember, a lifetime love of reading starts with a single step!

Visit us on the Web!
StepIntoReading.com
rhcbooks.com

Educators and librarians, for a variety of teaching tools, visit us at
RHTeachersLibrarians.com

Library of Congress Cataloging-in-Publication Data is available upon request.
ISBN 978-0-593-43250-1 (trade) — ISBN 978-0-593-43251-8 (lib. bdg.)

Printed in the United States of America
10 9 8 7 6 5 4 3 2 1

This book has been officially leveled by using the F&P Text Level Gradient™ Leveling System.

CORDUROY
Writes a Letter

by Alison Inches
illustrated by Allan Eitzen
based on the characters created by Don Freeman

Random House 🏠 New York

Lisa took a big bite out of

her cookie.

"Something's different.

I know what it is.

It doesn't have enough sprinkles!"

"Why don't you write a letter to the bakery?" said her mother.

"Good idea!" said Lisa.

She got out a pen and a pad of paper.

She stared at the pad.

The clock went

Tick tick.

Tick tick.

After a while, she said,

"What's the use, Corduroy?

The baker will not listen to me.

I'm just a little girl."

She put down her pen and left.

Maybe I can write a letter, thought

Corduroy.

Dear Mr. Baker:

We love your cookies.

We buy them every week.

Today there were fewer sprinkles.

We thought you should know.

From,

Corduroy

Corduroy put the letter

in the mailbox.

The next week, Lisa and Corduroy
picked up the cookies.

"Look, Corduroy!" said Lisa.

"The cookies have more sprinkles!"

"That's right!" said the baker.

"Someone sent me a letter."

THEATER

That night, Lisa and her mother went to the movies.

Corduroy went, too.

"Hey, look at the sign!" said Lisa.

"The lights are out on two of the letters."

"Why don't you write the owner a letter?" said her mother.

"Maybe I will," said Lisa.

15

Later, Lisa got a pen and a pad
of paper.

"What should I write, Corduroy?"
asked Lisa.

Soon she began to feel sleepy.

"It's no use," said Lisa.

"The movie theater owner is
too important.

He will not read a letter from me."

She went to bed.

But Corduroy was not
ready for bed.

I can write a letter, he thought.

20

THEATER

A few days later, Lisa and her mother walked past the movie theater.

Lisa looked at the sign.

"It's all fixed!" she said.

"That's neat," said Lisa.
"The next time I have something
to say, I'm going to
write a letter."

Every day, Lisa listened to music

on the radio.

Corduroy listened, too.

"I love this new radio station,"

said Lisa.

"But I wish they would play the
song 'Teddy Bear Bop.'
I should write to the station
and ask them to play it," said Lisa.
Great idea! thought Corduroy.

Lisa got her pen and pad.

She wrote:

Dear WROC:

I listen to your station every day.

I wish you would play

"Teddy Bear Bop."

I love that song.

My bear Corduroy loves it, too.

Thanks for being

the best station ever.

Yours truly,

Lisa

Lisa put the letter

in the mailbox.

The next week,

Lisa had the radio on.

The person on the radio
said, "This next song is for
Corduroy from Lisa."
Then "Teddy Bear Bop"
began to play.
Lisa and Corduroy danced
around the room.

"Wow!" said Lisa.

"They're playing our song!"

See, thought Corduroy.

It pays to write letters!